Louisiana

Native Americans

A Kid's Look at Our State's Chiefs, Tribes, Reservations, Powwows, Lore, and More From The Past and the Present

By Carole Marsh

NATIVE AMERICAN HERITAGE ™

Graphic Design: Lynette Rowe • Cover Design: Victoria DeJoy

Published by

GALLOPADE™
INTERNATIONAL

800-536-2GET
www.gallopade.com

Gallopade is proud to be a member of these educational organizations and associations:

The National School Supply and Equipment Association (NSSEA)
American Booksellers Association (ABA)
Virginia Educational Media Association (VEMA)
Association of Partners for Public Lands (APPL)
Museum Store Association (MSA)
National Association for Gifted Children (NAGC)
Publishers Marketing Association (PMA)
International Reading Association (IRA)
Association of African American Museums (AAAM)

Native American Heritage™ Series

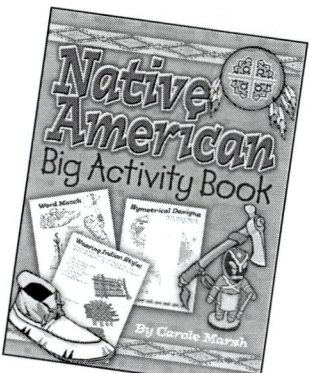

Native American
Big Activity Book

Native American
Biographies

Native American
Coloring Book

Native American
Heritage Book

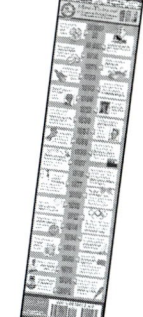

Native American
Timeline

Louisiana STATE STUFF™

My First Pocket Guide: Louisiana

My First Book About Louisiana

Louisiana Coloring Book

The Big Louisiana Reproducible Activity Book

Jeopardy: Answers & Questions About Our State

Louisiana "Jography!": A Fun Run Through Our State

Louisiana Gamebooks

Louisiana Bingo Games

Louisiana Illustrated Timelines

Louisiana Project Books

Louisiana Bulletin Board Set

Louisiana PosterMap

Louisiana Stickers

Let's Discover Louisiana! CD-ROM

Word from the Author

Hello!

I hope you are as interested in North America's wonderful Indian heritage as I am!

Like most kids, I grew up thinking of Indians as the other half of Cowboys. Today, of course, we are getting a much clearer and more accurate picture of what the first peoples on our land were all about. These "facts" are much more fascinating than anything Hollywood can make up. And you probably won't find much of this information in your history textbook!

I am 1/16 Cherokee. This is something I am very proud of and happy about. My grandmother was 1/4 Cherokee. She had tan skin, long gray hair and a very Indian look – especially if I did something bad! Her maiden name was Carrie Corn. Of course, when she got married, she took her husband's name, so it was many years before I learned to appreciate the significance of my native heritage.

Today, I'm trying to make up for lost time by exploring my roots as deeply as I can. One of the most interesting things I've learned is how fascinating all of the Indian tribes are – in the past, the present and future!

As you read about "your" Indians, remember that all native peoples were part of an ever-changing network of time, ideas, power and luck — good and bad. This is certainly a history that is not "dead," but continues to change – often right outside our own back doors! – all the time.

Carole Marsh
She-Who-Writes

PS: Many references show different spellings for the same word. I have tried to select the most common spelling for the time period described. I would not want to be in an Indian spelling bee!

is for . . .

Adze

An Indian woodworking tool used to cut, scrape, or gouge; often used to hollow dugout canoes. Blades were made of stone, shell, bone or copper.

Avoyelles

Means "the vipers." Tribe that once lived near the Red River in Louisiana.

Awl

An Indian's "needle." Often made from wood, thorns, bone, or metal, it was used to punch holes in skins so they could be sewn together.

Atakapa

An extinct tribe of Indians. Belonged to the Siouan language family. Once lived near Middle or Prien Lake in Louisiana. Their name meant "Man-Eaters" in Choctaw. Said to have been cannibals who ate the flesh of their enemies!

Apalachee

This farming tribe's homelands were in the Florida panhandle. Built mounds with temples on top. After the Spanish lost Florida in the French and Indian war, many Apalachee migrated to Louisiana, settling along the Red River.

Altar

A platform made of rocks or animal skulls; some had bowls, feathers, rattles, or skins on them. Indians prayed at these altars for things like good crops or expert hunting skills.

Arrow

A long, slender shaft made of reed, cane, or wood; pointed tip was attached to one end and split feathers to the other. Feathers helped the arrows fly straight.

Arrowhead

The pointed tip of an arrow, made of bone, antler, wood, or iron. Some tips had barbs that would embed themselves in flesh. These barbs made it difficult for an enemy to remove the arrowhead from a wound.

Alabama

This tribe was part of the Creek Confederacy. Many left their homelands in Alabama after the French and Indian War (around 1763), and a group of them settled north of New Orleans along the Mississippi River.

Aborigine

A member of the earliest known population of a region.

5

B is for . . .

Biloxi

Small Siouan-speaking tribe. They met the expedition to Louisiana to establish the first French colony and furnished the names for the first 2 capitals of Louisiana, Old and New Biloxi. A few still live in Rapides Parish, Louisiana, but the tribe is almost extinct.

Band

A subdivision of an Indian tribe. In earlier times, a band was sometimes created when part of a tribe split off from the main group. The band also chose new leadership.

Blankets

Used for door covers, partitions, bags, to dry food on, carry babies and many other purposes.

Baton Rouge

According to legend, the Houmas and Bayougoulas Indians staked off separate hunting grounds by smearing a tall cypress pole with animal blood. When early explorers saw this, they named it Baton Rouge, meaning "red stick."

Burial Practices

The Choctaw of Louisiana cleaned the bones of the dead and put them in boxes and baskets in their bone houses. Certain members of the tribe grew long fingernails for the purpose of cleaning the bones.

Baskets

Some were woven and others were coiled. Baskets were made from roots, grasses, barks, and other natural materials.

Bayou

This name means sluggish stream that forms the inlet or outlet of a lake or bay, connects two bodies of water, or a branch of a river flowing through a delta. It is from the Choctaw word bayuk, which means "small river."

Bow

Made from wood, horn or bone. Louisiana Indian children learned how to use bows. The bowstring was made from animal gut, rawhide or twisted vegetable fibers.

Beads

Made of wood, shells, claws, minerals, seeds — you name it! Later, the Louisiana Indians traded with white men for glass beads, used in some of their decorative arts.

6

Coushatta

Some of this tribe migrated west to Louisiana after the French and Indian War, in 1763. Today there is a community near Kinder, and a reservation at Elton.

Chief

Leader of a tribe. Different titles meant different things. Some members were made chief because they owned deeds to land. Chieftainship was often inherited, usually from the mother!

Contact Period

What historians call the era in the 1500s when Native Americans first met Europeans. This meeting changed the lifestyle of the Louisiana Indians more than anyone could ever have anticipated!

Chitimacha

This tribe's ancestral territory was in the lower part of Louisiana. Famous for their beautiful baskets and their silverwork. A small community of them can be found at Charenton.

Choctaw

Largest tribe of the southern Muskhogean-speaking Indians. Farming Indians. Their name meant "flat" because of their custom of flattening their heads. They were friendly to early French settlers in Louisiana. They were always at peace with America and ceded most of their lands to the U.S. government.

Confederacy

A union of different groups of people. A confederacy in Indian culture was a group of tribes that agreed not to fight with each other. They agreed to live peacefully. Sometimes the tribes shared culture and language.

Clan

A tribal unit. Members are descended from the same ancestor.

Citizenship

The Indian Citizenship Act of 1924 states all Indians born in the United States are citizens of the United States, and citizens of the states they live in, even though they may live on a reservation. They can vote. They pay most local, state and federal taxes, including sales taxes.

Caddo

Indian tribe whose members had dark skin and were of medium height. They pierced their noses, wore rings in them and tattooed their skin. They lived in cone-shaped grass lodges. Originally lived in the Red River part of Louisiana. A parish in our state is named for them.

Creek

Creek Indians could be found in eastern Louisiana before they were removed to Indian Territory in the 1830s. The Creek tribe consisted of many different bands and villages. Together with other small tribes, they were part of the Creek Confederacy.

7

Dance

There were Indian dances for every occasion: war, peace, hunting, rain, good harvests, etc. Drums, rattles, and flutes of bone or reed provided the music. Dancers often chanted or sang while performing. Steps were not easy to learn and required consistent practice.

Descendants

The first Louisiana Indians were descendants of primitive hunters who crossed the Bering Strait from Asia to what is now Alaska. At that time, glacial ice still covered most of North America. These people were the true discoverers of the "New World!"

Drum Dance

This dance was performed by the Caddo Indians. It was only performed in the evening. Through song and dance, it told the Caddo creation story.

Disease

Louisiana Indians had no immunity to the diseases that white explorers, colonists and settlers brought to their lands. These diseases included smallpox, measles, tuberculosis and others, which ravaged the tribes in great epidemics that killed many, and sometimes all, members of a tribe.

Dyes

Made of lichens, berries, roots, bark, plants, and other natural materials by Indians in Louisiana. Different colors were used depending on what materials were available and what objects were to be dyed.

Dishes

Made from clay, bark, wood, stone, and other materials, depending on what was available and what food they would be used for.

Doustioni

Caddo band that once lived on Louisiana's Red River.

Dreams

Important in the Indian tradition. It was believed that dreams were the "windows" to the soul. Many thought a person's hidden desires were expressed in dreams.

8

Eagle

An animal used in many Indian ceremonies. Eagle feathers attached to war bonnets and shields communicated an Indian's rank in his tribe and what kinds of deeds he had done. Feathers also adorned rattles, pipes, baskets, and prayer sticks.

Effigy Mound Culture

Built earthen figures of birds, animals or people.

Early Indians

In the 1600s and 1700s, several Indian groups lived in Louisiana in the swamps, forests and prairies. The Tunica had villages in the northeastern corner of the state. The Muskhogean-speaking tribes lived north of Lake Pontchartrain. The Caddo lived in the northwest. The Atakapa and Chitimacha lived in the south. Each of these main groups was divided into smaller groups; each had its own language.

Education

The Louisiana Department of Education has an Indian Education Program operated out of Baton Rouge.

Earrings

Medicine men sometimes pierced male and female ears at special ceremonies. Earrings, which cost parents or relatives a significant amount, symbolized wealth and distinction. The more earrings that an Indian wore, the greater his honor. Some earrings measured 12 inches in length!

Environment

Preserving the environment is important to preserving Native American heritage. For thousands of years, Native American tribes lived completely off the land. Farming, mining, pollution have all had a part in changing native environments.

English

In the 1800s, the U.S. government built boarding schools for Indian children throughout the nation. Children were forced to leave their homes and families to live at these schools. They were required to learn English and not speak their native languages.

Epidemics

Few Indians possessed immunity to the deadly diseases, like smallpox and measles, which European explorers and settlers brought to the New World. As a result, great population loss took place. Sometimes entire tribes became extinct. Epidemics sparked by Hernando De Soto's expedition are estimated to have killed 75% of the native population in the New World.

9

F is for . . .

Fetish

These small objects were thought to hold the spirit of an animal or a part of nature. A fetish could be an object found in nature, such as bone or wood, or it could be a carved object. The fetish was usually small enough to be carried in a small bag or on a cord. The making and use of a fetish was kept secret by its owner and only shared with the one who inherited it.

Fishers

Early Louisiana peoples hunted and gathered to keep from starving. Later, they learned to fish. When they finally learned to farm crops, they were more able to settle down into villages, instead of needing to forage all the time.

Furniture

Louisiana Indian furniture was very simple. Beds were made of skins laid over a frame of wooden slats; the bed posts were driven into the ground. There was often a storage place over the bed to keep personal items.

Fire Drill

A device used by Indians to make fires which consisted of a stick and a piece of wood with a tight hole in it. The stick was twirled rapidly in the hole, creating friction that would ignite shredded grass or wood powder placed nearby to start a fire.

Farmers

Many Louisiana Indians, ancient and modern, have farming ways! Even pre-contact Indians tilled and irrigated, raising many important crops. Corn, cotton, beans, squash, melons, sunflowers, gourds, pumpkins and tobacco are all native Indian crops!

Federal Recognition

The United States government's official acknowledgement of a group of Indians as a tribe that is eligible for government benefits, programs and funds.

Footwear

Louisiana Indians wore different footwear depending on their tribe and environment. Moccasins were made mostly of animal skin. Sandals were made of rawhide or plant material.

First on the Land

While many Indian groups rose up, then died out over many thousand years, we know little about the earliest groups, since they left no written records. European explorers left records of the Indians who followed these peoples in the 1600s and 1700s.

is for . . .

Games

Adults played ball and other games of chance or skill. Indian children spun tops, fought pretend battles, did target-shooting, walked on stilts, played hide and seek, or competed to see who could hold their breath the longest!

Governor's Commission on Indian Affairs

Located in Baton Rouge.

Grosse Tete

Chitimacha Indian village in Louisiana. Their name means "big head."

Gens

Group of related members from different tribes.

Gathering

Native Americans gathered natural materials for food, fuel, baskets, clothing, and housing. American Indians tribes also hunted to meet basic needs. Even though some tribes planted crops, most did some kind of gathering.

Gorgets

Beautiful ornaments hung around the neck or from ears; their significance, if any, is unknown.

Gourds

Hollowed-out shell of a gourd plant's dried fruit which often grew into a specific shape. Indians raised many species of gourds. They were used for spoons, bowls, masks, rattles, and even storage.

Grindstone Bluff Museum Library

Shreveport; collection of over 3,500 volumes, with an emphasis on Caddo and other area Indians.

is for . . .

Harrisonburg Indian Mound

Sacred ground of the Natchez or Ouachita tribes.

Hair

Indians used hair as a textile. Hair from bison, mountain sheep, elk, moose, deer, dog, rabbit, beaver, or even humans were used to weave cloth, make wigs, or stuff pillows, balls, dolls or drumsticks.

Horn and Hooves

Indians used animal horn to make spoons and dishes. Hooves were made into rattles and bird beaks were used for decoration.

Hopewell Culture

Early people who lived from about 100 B.C. to A.D. 500. Anthropologists believe they had a layered society with a defined organization and code of conduct. Because of this, they could work together to build great earthenworks called mounds. They also had an extensive trade network from the Midwest to the eastern U.S. seacoast.

Harvest

The Indians harvested wild rice by floating a canoe through the shallow water the rice grows in. The Indian bent the grain heads over into the canoe and hit them with a stick to cause the grain to fall into the boat.

Hunters

Early Indian peoples were hunters who used wooden spears with stone points to kill many kinds of large mammals that are extinct today, such as mammoths and mastodons!

Horses

Spaniards brought the horse to America. At first, Indians were afraid of the horse or thought it was sacred. Later, Indians "broke" horses gently, often "hypnotizing" them with a blanket. Horses were used for transportation, trade, barter or payment. Some Indians ate horse meat in hopes of yuining the animal's power.

Huma

Means "red people." Choctaw band that lived in Louisiana around 1699. Became extinct as a result of war and disease.

Houma Indian Communities

Indians who live in 6 communities in southeast Louisiana, including in Terrebonne and Lafourche parishes. Live primarily by trapping and fishing. But a growing number are leaving the bayous and going to cities to find work.

I is for . . .

Indian Scout

This term for a guide applied to Indians or white-skinned people who served that role.

Indian Reservation

A tract of land set aside by a government for Indians to live on.

Indian Removal Act of 1830

This federal act gave President Andrew Jackson the power to relocate tribes east of the Mississippi to an "Indian Territory." The forced removal of the southeast Indians later became known as the "Trail of Tears."

Independence

Native American tribes are sovereign nations. That means they are independent. Some even issue their own passports! However, Native Americans are also considered citizens of the United States and enjoy all the rights and privileges of U.S. citizens.

Indian Nation

The "Five Civilized Tribes" removed to Indian Territory were the Choctaw, Chickasaw, Creek, Seminole, and Cherokee. Each of these tribes was a part of the "Indian Nation," as the Indian Territory was called historically. Today, each of these tribes is a nation by itself. The old "Indian Nation" also included other tribes in the Gulf of Mexico states.

Indian Ladder

Indians made ladders by trimming branches off a tree. Some were left at consistent intervals to provide steps.

Indian Tribes in Louisiana

At one time or another, these tribes have lived in the state of Louisiana:
Alabama, Apalachee, Atakapa, Avoyelles, Biloxi, Caddo, Chitimacha, Choctaw, Coushatta, Creek, Natchez, Taensa, Tiou, Tunica, Yatasi

Indian

In 1493, Christopher Columbus called the native people he met in North America "Indians" because he mistakenly believed he had sailed to India! Today, this term includes the aborigines of North and South America.

J is for . . .

Just So You Know . . .

Today you can find many Louisiana Indians that follow some traditional ways. But there are also many who are entrepreneurs, doctors, lawyers, educators and even politicians! If you visit a reservation or cultural event, make sure you know visitor etiquette. Often dances are religious ceremonies and should be observed as such; religious dances should not be applauded. Photography, videotaping and drawing are all important issues – check with the tribe or individual before any is started.

Jesuits

Roman Catholic priests called Jesuits were among the first to meet and live with the North American Indians. Their writings, sent back to Europe, serve as one of today's best references to early Indian life.

Justice?

For hundreds of years, Native Americans have not received justice from federal and state governments. Native Americans have had nearly all their land taken away. Native Americans still have to fight for their rights in courts across the land.

Judicial Termination

Modern term to describe current efforts by various U.S. government agencies and officials (especially the judicial system) to legally decrease the sovereignty of independent Indian tribes.

Just In Time!

The Indian Arts and Crafts Act of 1990 makes it against the law to pretend that an item has been made by Native Americans if it is really not. It is illegal to offer or display for sale, or sell any art or craft product in a way that falsely suggests it is Indiun produced.

Jerked Meat

Thin strips of buffalo, elk, deer or other animal meat which is dried on racks in the sun; also called "jerky."

Kadohadacho

Caddo band. Friendly with the French. Met Spanish explorers near the Mississippi River in Louisiana in 1541.

Kill Site

An archaeological site where remains of many animals have been found along with human artifacts. Many kill sites have been useful to scientists in learning how ancient American Indians lived.

Killed Pottery

Pottery placed in a grave as an offering to the dead person was called killed pottery. A hole was formed in its base during creation. Often broken pottery was placed in a grave because Indians believed the spirit of the dead person would then be released and could travel.

Knife

Made from various materials such as bone, reed, stone, wood, antler, shell, metal, or animal teeth (bear, beaver, etc.), knives were used as weapons but also creative handiwork.

Knowledge

Knowledge is power. Native Americans shared knowledge with the first European settlers. Native Americans showed settlers how to plant crops, which plants were safe to eat, and other knowledge about the land.

Knots

Tied on bowstrings, spearhead and arrowhead lashings, snowshoes, and other items, knots were sometimes used to keep track of the days like a calendar—each knot equaled 1 day.

L is for . . .

Linguistic Families

There are 56 related groups of American Indian languages. A few of these speech families include Iroquoian, Algonquian, Siouan, Muskogean, Athapascan, and Wakashan.

Leggings

Both men and women wore cloth or skin covering, which were often decorated with quills, beads, or painted designs, for their legs.

Lost Tribes of Israel

This historic theory has been floating around since 721 BC. The 10 lost tribes of Israel are supposedly groups of people gathered together by Sargon, the King of Assyria. Some say he cast out 10 of the 12 tribes of Israel. Many have tried to prove that the American Indians are these missing tribes!

Lodge

The term for a type of Indian house that was usually a permanent dwelling. The population of a tribe was often estimated by its number of lodges.

Long Hairs

What their neighbors called the Choctaw because of the men's practice of letting their hair grow very long. Most Southeastern Indian men shaved their heads!

Land Loss

Native Americans lost their land in many ways. Conflicts with other tribes, colonization, European settlement, treaties, and removal took away Indian lands.

Lance

Spear used for hunting and war. The hunting lance had a short shaft and a broad, heavy head. The war lance was light and had a long shaft.

Lafayette Natural History Museum

Lafayette; see contemporary Indian baskets of the Chitimacha and Koasati Indians of Louisiana, and baskets and weaving of the Acadian culture and Louisiana Indian cultures.

Lariat

These throw ropes made of rawhide, buffalo hair, or horsehair sometimes measured up to 20 feet long!

Mobile Trade Language

Choctaw jargon used in trading along the Mississippi River. This language was also known as the Chickasaw Trade Language. The full Choctaw language was used as code during World Wars I and II.

Marksville State Commemorative Area

A group of earth mounds are located here, some in the form of truncated pyramids. These Indian villages were occupied from A.D. 100-400. A museum exhibits pottery shards, stone tools, pipes, animal bones and human bones.

Maize

Also called Indian Corn. Known as a "cereal" plant because it probably began as some form of grass. The Indians in our state figured out every possible way to use corn as a food. The only thing the white man added was the creation of "corn flakes!"

Medicine

Medicine could be good or bad. Medicines or charms were placed in a bag by young warriors and carried at all times. Some of the roots, leaves and bark that Indians in our state used as medicine are being rediscovered and used by today's doctors!

Muskhogean Family

Language family of Indians on the Gulf Coast states east of the Mississippi River and including Louisiana.

Mohongo

Wife of Chief Kihegashugah of the Osage Indian tribe. She was taken from New Orleans in 1827 and sent to France, where she and 2 other Indians were treated royally. However, all 3 Indians died from smallpox during the return voyage.

Mound Builders

About 2,000 years ago a wave of migrating people came to our area. They were the first of many groups to be known as the Mound Builders, for the earthenworks they created. Sometimes built high earthen walls around their villages, possibly for defense. They vanished long before the first white explorers reached Louisiana.

N is for . . .

Nomadic

A way of life in which people frequently moved from one location to another in search of food. "Seminomadic" people had permanent villages, but left them in certain seasons to hunt, fish, or gather wild plant foods.

Nacisi

Small Caddo band that lived in Louisiana around 1687.

Nation

There are many Indian nations located within the United States, such as the Caddo Nation. Indian nations are called nations because their governments and laws are independent of and separate from the U.S. government. The federal government must have "government to government" relations with these Indian nations, just as it would with foreign nations, like England or Spain.

November

In 1990, President George Bush approved a joint resolution designating November 1990 "National American Indian Heritage Month." Similar proclamations have been issued each year since 1994.

Names

Indian names were often changed during one's lifetime. These names could be derived from events that happened during the person's birth, childhood, adolescence, war service, or retirement from active tribal life. Some names came from dreams, some were inherited, and sometimes names were stolen or taken in revenge. Today some Indians maintain old, traditional Indian names, while others take modern names. Since settlers often did not read or write Indian languages, they recorded Indian names phonetically (as they "sounded"). Thus Indian names were often misspelled.

Natchez

Tribe with a unique and complex Meso-American caste system. The Natchez king was called the Great Sun, and was the absolute ruler. There were 3 classes of people: Royalty, Nobility, and Commoners. There were many strict rules about marriage and social rank. Mounds were built as temple bases. Tribe is noted for their death rituals for the upper classes, where the dead one's spouse and servants gave up their lives to accompany the him or her to the next world.

National Museum of the American Indian

The Smithsonian's National Museum of the American Indian on the National Mall in Washington, D.C., symbolizes a deeper understanding between America's first citizens and those who have come to make these shores their home.

Old Bones

No one knows for sure when the first people came to North America, but scientists have dated bones and artifacts discovered at Clovis, New Mexico around 11,200 years old. Testing on a skeleton found on the Channel Islands, off the coast of California showed they were about 13,000 years old. And, evidence of human habitation in southern New Mexico suggests that people may have been there as far back as 38,000 years ago.

Origins

Some scientists believe that Native Americans actually came across a land bridge between Asia and North America. They say that during an ice age thousands of years ago, the water level was much lower and people could have walked between the two continents.

Oil

Indians extracted oil from the many layers of fat that came with fresh bear meat. The fat was boiled down in earthen pots to produce the oil, which was stored in gourds and pots. The oil was used for cooking and even beautifying the body! Indians would mix red pigment with the oil, add the fragrances of cinnamon and sassafras, and rub it all over their bodies.

Orators

Many Indian leaders were excellent public speakers. Powerful and dramatic speakers were vital to leaders who wanted to influence their tribe. Watch for famous Indian quotations in literature and textbooks!

Office of Indian Education Programs

This is a service organization devoted to providing quality education opportunities for American Indian people. Established in the latter part of the nineteenth century to carry out the federal government's education commitment to Indian tribes, it has become the only national education system for American Indian children and adults.

P is for . . .

Powwow

The original form of the word meant "medicine man." Medicine men would often use noise motion and confusion to scare away harmful spirits and cure people. It was also a gathering to talk about political matters. Today, the powwow is an event where Indians gather to sing, perform ceremonial dances, and share cultural pride and traditions.

Pecan

Nut of the hickory tree, found in Louisiana river bottoms. Word comes from the Algonquian pakan, pukan or pagan which means "hard-shelled nut." It was highly-prized by the Indians.

Poverty Point

A large earthwork mound 3/4 of a mile in diameter. It rises up on 6 terraces to form a platform that may have been the foundation for dwellings. Located near Epps. Remnants of the earliest-known culture to exist in what today is Louisiana. The people who lived here around 3,000 years ago were farmers. They traded with groups as far away as the Ohio Valley. This civilization vanished around 700 B.C.

Pargoud Mound

Located near Monroe, Louisiana. Ceremonial center originally built by the Ouachita Indians.

Paint

Indians used many natural materials to make paint, like clay mixed with oil or grease. Yellow "paint" was made with the gall bladder of a buffalo! Why did they paint their faces or bodies? Indians used paint to look scary or beautiful, to disguise themselves, or to protect their skin from sunburn or insect bites. Indians often applied red paint because it symbolized strength and success. That is why settlers often referred to the Indians as Red Men.

Pemmican

Indian food made of animal meat, which was dried in the sun, pounded together with fat and berries. The mixture was packed into skin bags and used primarily while on the trail.

Picture History

Some Indians kept a record of time and important events by painting or drawing pictures or symbols on skin, bark, or stone.

Papoose

An American Indian infant aged between birth and one year is called a papoose. A papoose spent most of his or her days snugly wrapped in a kind of cradle made of skins or bark and a wooden frame that hung on the mother's back. This sturdy frame also allowed a mother to lean her papoose against a tree or rock within sight as she worked.

Pottery

Indian pottery was made from built-up spirals of clay that were molded or paddled, or a combination of the two methods. Most pottery served as cooking vessels.

is for . . .

Quillwork

Indians used the quills of porcupine or birds to make a type of embroidery. Quills were dyed with juice from berries and other materials. When they were ready to be used, the quills were either mashed with teeth or softened with hot water and flattened with rocks. The quills were then laced into moccasins, shirts, pipe covers, and other items. Beads which Indians received by trading with settlers eventually replaced quillwork.

Quality

Native American arts and crafts are known for their excellent craftsmanship and striking designs. This work is often influenced by things found in nature especially plants and animals.

Quiver

Case used to hold arrows; made of woven plant materials or animal skins.

Quirt

A short riding whip with a wood, bone, or horn handle.

Quarry Site

A location where Indians went for workable stone such as flint and made stone tools.

Rain Dancing

The rain dance ceremony, performed to encourage rainfall, was common among Indian religions because good weather is vital for a successful harvest. Rainmakers were in tune with nature; there are actual reported cases of Indians producing or preventing rain!

Roots

Indians used plant roots for food, medicine, dye, baskets, cloth, rope, salt, flavoring, and just to chew!

Rattles

Indians of Louisiana made rattles from bird beaks, animal hooves, bones, pods, seashells, turtle shells and other animal parts. The rattles are used in ceremonies.

Rawhide

Untanned animal hide. The "green" hide was stretched on the ground or over a frame. Flesh and fat were removed. The skin was dried, washed, then buried with wood ashes which made the hair come off. Used by the Louisiana Indian to make drumheads, lash lodge poles, mend broken objects and in many other ways.

"Red Sticks"

A warrior faction of the Creek Indians that lived in "red towns" was named Red Sticks by the settlers because of their red war poles. These Indians erected tall red poles in the village center when war was declared. These "red sticks" were in charge of men known as "bearers of the red." The warriors gathered around the poles to commit to the battle ahead.

Reservations

The U.S. government set aside, or "reserved," land for the Indians. These reservations originally served as a sort of prison during the beginning stages of Indian removal. At that time, reservations provided the government with some control over Indian activity and residency. This land was usually considerably less desirable land than the Indians' native territories. Today's reservations are lands that are tribally held, yet protected by the government.

"Red Towns"

Villages of the Red Stick Creeks. Called this or "Baton Rouges" for the red poles erected in the village that meant war!

S is for . . .

Sign Language

A way for Indians to communicate with others from a tribe whose language they did not speak.

Shaman

Medicine man and spiritual leader who was supposed to have special healing power from another world.

Secret Societies

Indians had secret groups, usually organized for religious or ceremonial reasons. Each society had a purpose, such as to cure disease.

Shield

A piece of "armor" made of a rawhide-covered frame, which was carried into battle. Shields also could be decorative and religious objects. Many tribes make shields today as an art form!

Sweatlodge

Structure used for ritual purification by sweating from exposure to very hot fires or hot steam from pouring water over hot stones. Also called a sweathouse, for some tribes also doubling as clubhouses.

Stone-boiling

Cooking method by placing preheated stones into cooking vessels.

Sacred Bundles

A group of objects treasured by a tribe. They were well-guarded and often taken into battle. The items were publicly shown only on very important occasions.

Saddle

While some Indians did use saddles on their horses, most rode bareback!

Spanish Moss

Used by the Louisiana Indians in cradles and for diapers!

Signals

Indian signs made with a pony, blanket, mirror, smoke, fire-arrow or other item to communicate over long distances.

Sachem

The supreme Indian ruler of an area where there are many related tribes.

23

is for . . .

Tobacco

A sacred plant early Indians used to make offering to their gods, cure diseases, bring good luck, seal agreements and bind treaties.

Treaties

Written agreements between the U.S. government and the Indians, most of which involved the Indians giving up their native lands.

Tiou

Indians that lived on the lower Mississippi and Yazoo Rivers in Louisiana in the early 1700s. Became extinct as a result of warfare.

Totem

The spirit of some natural object (usually an animal) taken by an Indian, tribe or family to guard over them.

Taensa

Indian tribe that once lived in northeastern Louisiana, later moving to the southwestern part of the state. The French reported that they practiced human sacrifice. A parish, river and bayou in Louisiana are named for them. Their tribe is believed to be extinct.

Tomahawk

A club, axe or hammer used to chop wood, drive stakes in the ground or as a weapon.

Tracking

To follow a trail by finding a sign such as a broken blade of grass, a moved stone or moccasin track. Indians learned to trail as children, so that they could find food, track enemies and disguise their own signs.

Teeth

Louisiana Indians hung teeth on cords to make necklaces.

Tribe

A group of Indians with shared culture, history, original territory, ancestry, social organization, and governmental structure. A tribe may contain several bands of Indians.

Tunica

This tribe's ancestral lands were near where the Mississippi and Yazoo Rivers join. They were farmers who also hunted, fished and gathered food. Noted for making a cloth fabric from the mulberry plant. Made pottery and dugout canoes. Mined salt to trade with other tribes. Started to gradually leave their homelands after the American Revolution. A group settled in Louisiana. Their descendants can be found today in the Tunica-Biloxi tribe.

Thunderbird

A mythological Indian figure, as well as a part of the constellations for many Indians. Thunderbird mythology is mostly different from tribe to tribe, in general either coexisting with ancestors as an actual bird, or appearing as a spiritual nature god. The Thunderbird was good to the people in either case. Much mythology ties the thunderbird with thunder, lightning and storms.

24

U is for . . .

U.S. Bureau of Indian Affairs

Provides public services such as law enforcement, land records, economic development, and education to Indians. Known for mismanagement and ethical problems.

U.S. Army

Many Native Americans have fought bravely for the United States Army. Many have also given their lives for a country that was not always accepting of them.

Unique

Each and every tribe has its own unique customs, language, and traditions.

U.S. Indian Schools

The Bureau of Indian Affairs operates hundreds of federal schools around the nation. Enrollment of Native American children measures in the thousands!

U.S. Indian Reorganization Act

Passed by Congress in 1934, the act authorized Indian tribes to establish and conduct their own governments, and to form businesses.

U.S. President

Once called Great White Father by Indians.

U.S. Colonists

Called Long Knives or Big Knives by early Indians, who also called English explorers "Coat Men."

U.S. Indian Wars

The U.S. War Department has compiled an official list of "Indian Wars" that occurred in the United States. Over 50 wars were fought between the U.S. and the Indians during the period of 1790-1850.

25

is for . . .

Vessels

Indians carried water in special gourds shaped liked bottles, called water vessels.

Village Councils

These were held in the town (council) house and occurred to discuss and decide important matters. Harmony and agreement was essential to tribal unity. Rather than vote on issues, they were discussed until everyone was satisfied. Anyone who wanted to could speak freely. Everyone did not always agree on the outcome, but everyone avoided conflict by pushing their case.

Vegetable Dyes

Indians could not buy color from the store like we can today. Instead, they created many different colors from the things they found on earth like plants, flowers, shrubs, trees, roots, and berries. They made beautiful and unique reds, oranges, yellows, greens, browns, and violets. These dyes were used for baskets, pottery, weaving, body makeup, and clothing.

Very Hungry

There were Indians who here hunters, gatherers and foragers, that often ate whatever they could find! How hungry would you have to be to eat what they sometimes ate: reptiles, larvae, and insects?

Villages

Many Louisiana Indians lived in villages! Villages were formed around different clans or bands within the tribe, but could also contain different clans living together. Villages were usually permanent settlements, although semi-nomadic tribes have been known to migrate between permanent villages.

Vesperic Indians

Indian tribes located in the United States.

is for . . .

Women

Indian women in some Louisiana tribes were poor and hardworking, like the men. But in some tribes, women had many rights, including becoming chief!

War Pony

Horse, often painted with colorful paint and ridden into battle.

War Bonnet

Special headdress worn into battle, often adorned with feathers.

War Dance

Indian braves danced this before going into battle. The dance was a way of assembling the braves and getting them to commit to the fight ahead.

Wampum

Algonquian word for "white." This described beads or strings of beads made of clam or whelk shells. They were used in trade between the Indians and settlers. In 1640, counterfeit wampum was made!

Whispering Wind

Bimonthly magazine of American Indian crafts; includes old photos, powwow dates and more. Published by Written Heritage in New Orleans.

Whistle

Indians from Louisiana made them from the wing bones of birds. The whistles made the sound of the bird the bones came from! Used to communicate, signal, sound an alarm or even flirt with a maiden!

White Man

Indians generally called them Pale Face, a name the white men themselves suggested!

War Club

A weapon made of stone, bone, or wood in the shape of a club.

Washa

Small band of Muskhogeans. Lived near New Orleans around 1699. By 1805, they were extinct.

XYZ are for . . .

Xenophobe

A xenophobe is someone who is afraid of foreign people, their customs and cultures, or foreign things. Many of the first European settlers were afraid of Native American cultures.

You Bet!

Some Native Americans say that Casinos make a lot of money. Others say that too many people have a gambling problem. In the 1980s and 1990s, many tribes discussed whether or not gambling casinos should be allowed. Now that many casinos have been built across the country, the debate has switched to how it should be controlled.

Yatasi

Tribe that once lived in Louisiana, part of the Caddo Confederacy. Friendly with the French. After a smallpox epidemic in 1805 and wars, they were reduced in numbers to less than 30 and moved to a reservation in Oklahoma.

ZZZZZZ...

Shamans and medicine men were not the only people who had access to the spirit world. Indians believed that people could make contact with spirits every night in their dreams! Dreamers could travel back to the time of man's creation or far ahead into their own futures. They also believed that dreams contained warnings or commands from the spirits. Many tribes felt that they had to act out their dreams as soon as they awoke. If an Indian dreamed about bathing, for example, he would run to his neighbors' houses first thing in the morning, and his neighbors would throw kettles full of cold water over him.

Yowani

Former Choctaw town; these Indians were moved to Louisiana around 1764.

Y... Or, "Why?"

1. Why do you think Indian warriors carried charms with them? Some Indian medicines have been scientifically proven to have true healing power and are still used today. Do you think their charms had any real power to help them win battles?
2. Why do you think the American government kept relocating Indians onto reservations and then making the reservations smaller and smaller?
3. Why did Indians use items such as a pipe in ceremonies? What kinds of symbolic objects do we use in ceremonies today?
4. Why and how did Indians use natural materials in creative ways?
5. Many Indian tribes are running successful businesses on their reservations today. There is one industry that many tribes are making a lot of money at. Do you know what this is? Hint:"I'll bet you do!"

28

Which Famous Native American Am I?

Solve the puzzle!

Down

1. This Shoshone woman joined Lewis and Clark as their guide and translator and helped make the expedition a success! Hint: She has 4 "a"s in her name!

4. This man gave the Cherokee their first alphabet so that they could write. Until then, they communicated only by speaking and drawing pictures. Hint: A famous ancient tree also has the same name!

5. He was one of the fiercest of Indian warriors! He fought against white settlers in Arizona and New Mexico to keep his people from being pushed off their lands. Hint: Jump!

Word Bank

Black Elk	Crazy Horse	Sitting Bull	Sequoia
Sacajawea	Chief Joseph	Geronimo	Pocahontas

Across

2. A legend says that this brave Algonquian woman saved the life of Englishman John Smith. Hint: Disney produced a movie about her.

3. He fought at Little Bighorn when he was only 13! He was also a wise "shaman" who saw visions and could advise people. Hint: Part of his name is an animal with antlers!

6. He was a great Sioux warrior who won the battle against General Custer at Little Bighorn in 1876. Hint: His horse was not crazy!

7. A leader of the Lakota (Sioux) tribe who lived on the Standing Rock Reservation in North Dakota after the battle of Little Bighorn. He tried to make conditions better for his people there, so the U.S. government called him a "troublemaker." Hint: He did not sit all the time!

8. A wise and brave chief of the Nez Percé who tried to bring his people to Canada to escape war. He said, "From where the sun now stands, I will fight no more forever." Hint: His father's name was "Old Joseph."

Different Ways for Different Indians!

North American Indian tribes are divided into different areas. In each of these areas, tribes shared common ways of living with each other. They might make similar arts or crafts, they might eat the same foods, or they might have had the same beliefs. These activities are all part of their "culture." Each area had its own culture, which was different from the tribes in all the other areas.

Below is a map of all the different groups of Indian tribes in North America. Color each area with a different color. You will see a colorful picture of how Native Americans can all be called "Indians" but still have very different cultures!

ARCTIC

ARCTIC

ARCTIC

ARCTIC

ARCTIC

SUBARCTIC

SUBARCTIC

NORTHWEST COAST

PLATEAU

GREAT PLAINS

NORTHEAST

GREAT BASIN

CALIFORNIA

SOUTHEAST

SOUTHWEST

MESOAMERICA

CARIBBEAN

Celebration!

Powwows are big festivals where Native Americans gather to sing, dance, and eat together. It is a time to celebrate and show pride in their culture. Powwows can last from one afternoon to several days. The Indians dress in native costumes and dance ancient dances to the beating of drums.

Artists sell their arts and crafts. You might be able to buy some real Native American food cooked on an open fire. Native Americans go to powwows to be with each other, share ideas, and just have fun! Most powwows are also open to people who are not Indian. It's a great place to learn about Native American culture!

If you went to a powwow this weekend, what do you think you would see? What do you think might NOT be there? Circle the objects you think you would see at a powwow. Put an X through those you probably won't see.

©2004 Carole Marsh/Gallopade International/www.gallopade.com/Louisiana Indians A-Z

Make an Indian Weaving!

Many Native Americans used weaving to create useful things like sashes (belts), bags, mats, and blankets. They used animal hair to make yarn, and dyed the yarn with natural dyes from fruits and other plants. They also used some plant fibers, like cotton, to make weaving thread.

Weave a small Native American mat of your own. Use different colors of yarn to create a beautiful pattern in your weaving. Place a favorite object on the mat or hang it on your wall!

Prepare the "loom"

Cut a piece of cardboard 5 inches wide and 6 inches long. Along the two 5-inch sides (the "short" sides), have an adult cut slits 1/4 inch deep. These slits should be 1/2 inch apart from each other. So, on each short side you will have 9 slits.

Directions:

1. Take a long piece of yarn and bring it from the back through the first slit (the one next to the edge of the cardboard.) The end of the yarn will hang down behind the cardboard.

2. Bring the yarn right across the front of the cardboard to the slit opposite the one your yarn came through.

3. Now bring the yarn under the back of the cardboard and then up again through the second slit.

4. Repeat #2 and #3, until you have 9 strands of yarn across the front of your cardboard!

5. Then cut the yarn and tie the two loose ends in the back of the cardboard.

6. Take another piece of yarn and start feeding it through the 9 strands, going over one, under the next over the next, etc. When you get to the end, pull the yarn behind the cardboard and around to the front, and begin again. This time, whatever strand you went over, go under. And whatever strand you went under, go over.

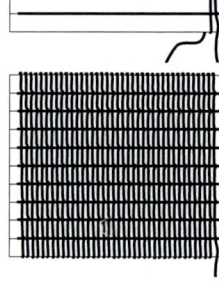

7. Repeat this pattern until the front of your cardboard in covered. Then cut the yarn in the back of the cardboard, and trim it to create a fringe for your mat!

Tips:
- For a wild look, use variegated or different colored yarn!
- For a tighter mat, push the under/over strands up against the previous strands during weaving.
- To keep your mat from unravelling, tie neighboring fringe together up close to the mat.

Finders Keepers?

Native Americans have many buried treasures. For hundreds of years, special objects would sometimes be buried with Native Americans, or maybe they would just be lost. Archeologists used to dig for interesting artifacts in old Native American gravesites. They would keep the Native American bones or the arrowheads, rattles, masks and other objects that they found. But this made the Native Americans feel like they were being robbed.

In 1990, the U.S. government passed a law that said that no one could look for or take these Native American objects anymore. And whoever had any already had to give them back to the people they belonged to. This is called repatriation

Help the archeologist return the artifact to a Native American.

FINISH

START

Fast Fact

An artifact is an object that was made by people a long time ago for some useful purpose.

Busy Hands!

Before modern times, Native Americans didn't have stores where they went to buy things. They made everything they needed.

What did Indians make with their own hands? Use the Word Bank and pictures to find out!

Word Bank

blanket	moccasins	arrows	pottery	canoe
mat	food	jewelry	pouch	box

_ _ _ _ _ _ _ _ _ _ _ _ _ _

_ _ _ _ _ _ _ _ _ _ _ _ _ _

_ _ _ _ _ _ _ _ _ _ _ _

_ _ _ _ _ _ _ _

_ _ _ _ _ _ _ _ _ _ _ _ _ _

_ _ _ _ _ _ _ _ _

_ _ _ _ _ _ _

_ _ _ _ _ _

American Indians Today

Beginning with the first letter of each group of letters, cross out every other letter to discover some new words. You may not have heard of these before, but you can read all about them!

1. Many Indians live on these, but many more do not!

TRYELSDEBRNVJAOTPIPOWNASX

_____

2. Many Indians have been poor for a long time because for many years the government took away their lands and their ability to make a living.

TPKOOVWEBRNTXYA

_____

3. Many Indians have been studying hard at school and going to college in order to earn more money. Education helps the Indians make their lives better. These Native Americans are working to become:

TSJUMCBCFEYSMSOFPUVL

_____

4. This is a big term that means Native Americans have worked hard to get the U.S. government to let them rule themselves. This means that they have their own laws and make their own decisions. They are like a separate country inside the U.S.! Now, try and see if you can get your parents to give you the same thing!

TSGENLBF   **JDGEETSEWRAMCIHNUAKTYIKOTNU**

_____   _____

Fast Fact
What do Indians work as today?

- doctors   • artists
- nurses   • lawyers
- factory workers   • actors

The same kinds of jobs any
American might work at!

35

Native Americans Move to the City!

Solve the code to discover the mystery words!

A	B	C	D	E	F	G	H	I	J	K	L	M
✳	❁	✕	♣	➔	♥	❗	✴	✂	✆	☛	✍	✉

N	O	P	Q	R	S	T	U	V	W	X	Y	Z
❀	☆	◆	✡	✐	✇	☎	✒	✚	✘	☁	✠	✓

1. During the 1950s and 1960s, the American government paid Indians to leave their homes on reservations and move to cities to get jobs. If cities are sometimes called urban areas, then these brave Indians were called:

2. Many Indians chose to stay on their reservations and not move to the city. They thought that if they moved to the city, they would lose the way of life that their parents and ancestors had taught. These Indians called themselves:

3. Native Americans who moved to cities lived close to each other. They tried to keep their way of life as much as possible. They did not want to forget their religion, native art, or music. They did not want to lose their:

4. Are you afraid of heights? Many people are. The Mohawk Indians are not! Many of them work hundreds of feet above the city to build steel frames for skyscrapers. People who do this work above the city are:

5. Today urban Indians and reservation Indians come together to celebrate their culture. They share ideas and stories. They dance and beat drums. They make and sell Indian jewelry. During these celebrations, Indians remember how much they have to be proud of! These big parties are called

36